P9-BZX-645

Her slim brown hands
What is it they make?
Needle flying and time too,
In the candlelight, in the candlelight.
Stitch, stitch, stitch,
She's stitching up the dark with hope,
This pretty shape and that
In her lonely nighttime light.
Stitch, stitch, stitch,
What is it they make, her hands,
As they work on through the night?
Stitch, stitch, stitch,
Stitch, stitch, stitch,
In the candlelight, in the candlelight.

Sky Sash
So Blue

by Libby Hathorn   illustrated by Benny Andrews

Simon & Schuster Books for Young Readers

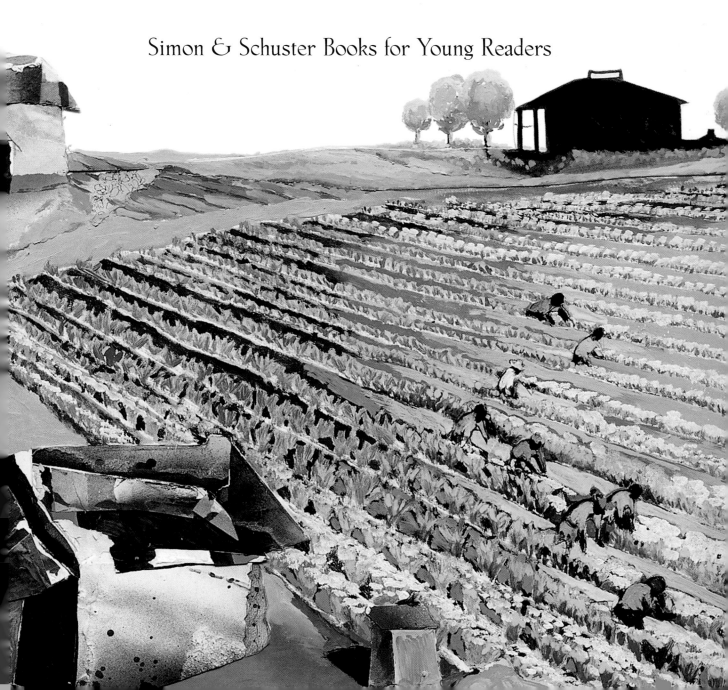

In a secret box, in a secret place,
A child keeps a thing so fine,
A sash of pale blue, made of pieces of sky,
Her Ma'am stitched together, a fine silky tie,
A small gift of fabric, so smooth and so brave,
She scarcely believes that it's hers—
Such a sash for Susannah—a slave!

She often takes it out to play
Late night to twirl and twine,
But soon there'll be a special day
When she'll *wear* that sash so fine.
"Blue sash, oh blue sash,
Oh, I love you true sash."
She smooths it with soft caress—
"I have you, oh blue sash,
My sky blue, my true sash,
But my big sister Sissy,
Must have her a dress,
Must have her an all-over dress!"

They've been collecting for weeks,
In the Big House
Where they've worked forever,
They've been collecting for weeks,
Mother and daughters together.
A duster rag from the kitchen
Of pretty cotton blue,
Then a cast-off piece of petticoat
That the Missus ripped in two.
They've been collecting for weeks,
Some muslin for covering cheese,
A piece of linen for polishing glass,
A patch of chamois, if you please . . .
They've been collecting for weeks
From rag-piles, cast-off mess
For Mother and daughters determined
Sissy will have her all-over dress.

First the bodice,
Small and neat for Sissy to try,
Then sleeves so puffed and pretty,
Could make a person cry.
And piece by piece that swishing skirt
To swing, to swirl, to fly!
A scrap of net, outrageous, light,
Round Sissy's neck, this flimsy tie.
Susannah laughs at the very sight,
Her sister looks so pleased, so shy.

This pretty shape and that pretty patch
In those strong brown hands they meet,
Needle flying against the time,
For they have a meeting to keep.
John Bee's coming from far away
And he'll be here on a special day.
"It will be finished," their Ma'am says,
As she fits a scrap of flannel,
"It's all but done, 'cept for the skirt,
Not a thing to hand for that last back panel.
We just keep looking, where we may—
I reckon we'll find it any old day!"

"Blue sash, oh blue sash,
It's hard to do sash
But it's *you* must finish
My big sister's dress.
I'm sorry as sorry
That you have to go,"
Susannah takes it to Sissy
But Sissy says, "No!
It's your sash to wear,
Your sky sash so blue
Stitched by our Ma'am,
It was made for you!"

"Good luck, oh blue sash,
Good luck you must bring.
You piece of sky
My hope won't die
We'll find it, I know it,
That last bit for Sissy
Just the right thing!"

Susannah waits and looks
And her heart skips a beat—
It's been scorched by the fire
The Missus' white sheet.
"Cut it up girl, for rags, girl,
we need a fresh pile.
Cut it up girl, for rags."
She's glad to oblige.
She hides her hands for
They shake with pleasure
As she throws down the sheet,
Makes a secret measure,
Then she cut, cut, cuts,
Shape those dusters so fine.
"Why you smiling that way?
Sitting over that sheet?"
Don't answer! Oh don't!
But one of these dusters
Be ours to keep.

Late night in their place
Laugh, talk and sew—
Shake out a new dress
That only they know.
Off with the old, and
On with the new,
Sissy swirling and laughing
At last it's come true.
Then the flat iron's weight
To smooth and press
This work of cloth,
Sissy's special dress!
This out of next−to−nothing
That's to be her *wedding dress*!

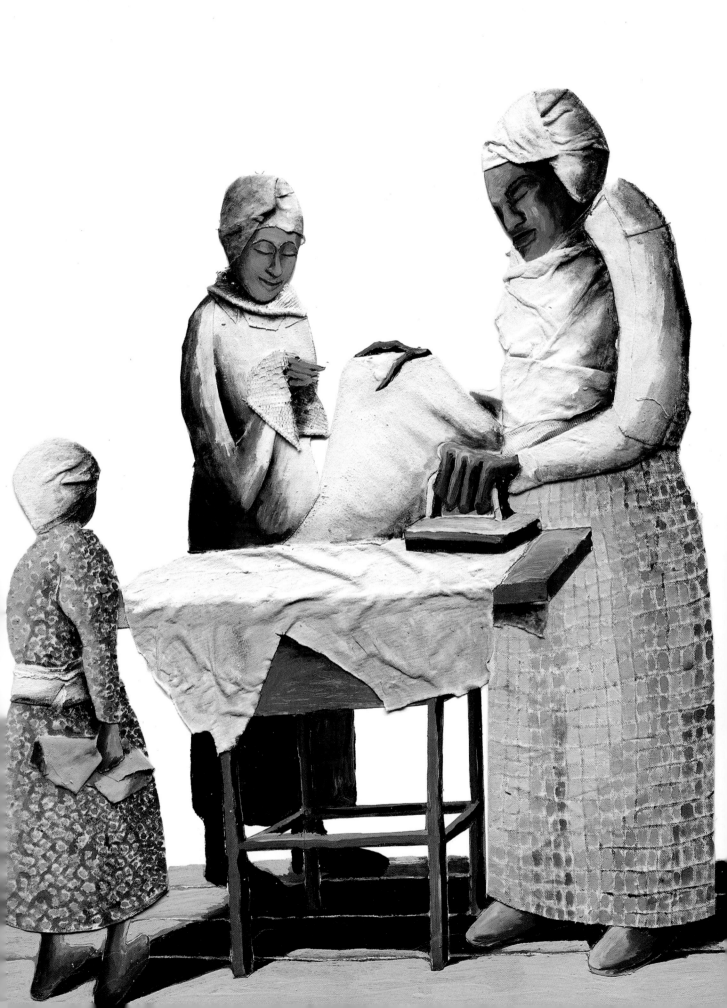

When her John Bee comes walking fast,
From his paying job so far away,
When her John Bee comes walking fast
Then it's to be her wedding day!
And quick as he can, and soon, as soon,
For Sissy's freedom that man will pay!

They're not allowed a preacher,
Susannah knows her mother tried—
The Missus only laughs, asks why?
"Slaves don't need a preacher!"
Their mother has her pride.
She decides *she'll* be the one
To pray them, sing and bless
For she's miracl'd something already
And out of next−to−nothing
Stitched a wedding dress.

In the field beyond the barn
The hour of happiness,
The corn stalks bow down,
Bow down to Sissy's dress,
And to the sash so blue,
"You beautiful to see," they sigh
"You beautiful, it's true!"
"Just a few months more," John Bee says
As their mother smiles and sings and prays.

And so they marry each other, there,
And the rustling wind gives praise.

Susannah watches the couple laugh and dance
But later her sister will cry—
It doesn't seem fair, on their wedding day,
The two just married must kiss good-bye.
Over and over, loving and strong
John Bee promises it won't be too long.
"Sissy, that dress and how you wear it!
On your freedom day, believe me,
I'll return for you, I swear it!"
"Go back now," their mother sighs,
"There's no more time to talk—
You'll lose your job John Bee,
If you don't make that lonesome walk!"

Susannah takes her sister's hand,
"What a wedding day, such a wedding day!"
So many things hard to understand.
"What a wedding day, such a wedding day!"
Their Ma'am talks loud to hide her sorrow,
"Now go to your bed, both you good girls
Work by the plenty for us tomorrow!"

"What a wedding day, such a wedding day.
My sash so blue, her dress so fine
How come I had me such a sad happy time?"

The house is quiet
The two girls sleep,
Then snip, snap, snip,
One jumps to her feet,
And soft as first rain
In this night so deep,
Susannah hears
Her mother weep.
Hears that snip, snap, snip.
Sees the scissors fly.
"Missus was askin'
'Bout her duster put by
From that burnt-up sheet?"
And pieces of dress
Cast down on the floor
Just rags now, flung in a heap.

"Sometimes it seems like everythin' goes,"
Her mother never cries for long,
"It seems like everyone, everythin' goes."
But tonight her voice is bitter-strong.
So tonight Susannah tells her Ma'am, "No!
Some things stay fast, don't ever go.
Out of nothing you made something,
Something never to forget—
Clean out of next-to-nothing
You made our Sissy her wedding dress!"

In Missus' house a duster found,
I'm the wedding dress, I'm the wedding dress
Susannah dusts it up, keeps her laughing down.
In the kitchen, jelly net spilled through fingers
I'm the wedding dress, I'm the wedding dress
In the gloom of the parlor a moment she lingers
"You in luck, polishin' rag goin' round,"
I'm the wedding dress, I'm the wedding dress
"For didn't you dance, skirt swirling, spreading,
Didn't you dance at my sister's wedding?"

In the hall Missus' daughter rustles by
In a dress, oh all-over silky blue!
And Susannah remembers another dress
And the way her mother's fingers flew.
She dusts, she sweeps, smooths and rubs
She shines and polishes, smiles as she scrubs,
Up and down Missus' house, in and out Missus' house
Hard work Susannah won't care—
Those patches and pieces, day after day,
That wedding dress is everywhere!

When he comes for Sissy, John Bee,
Susannah knows she should be glad
But she can't help it, just can't help it
Her brow, her lips, her eyes act sad.
"He's coming back for us, John Bee,"
Ma'am tells Susannah so bright,
"He's a fine good man, in a year or two
He'll buy our freedom, it'll be all right.
Now hug your sister once more child,
No crying, no sighing this farewell night."

But there's one last thing,
Before the pair go
Susannah decides she must do,
She runs to get it, for Sissy to take it,
The wonder sash, so silky blue,
And once again Sissy tells her no
But this time her Ma'am says yes,
"Take it, to think back on us here,
'Bout your wedding day, your wedding dress.
This gift of Susannah's will tie us fast,
No matter how long till we meet again,
This sash says our love got to last."

Late night by the fire,
Feeling sorry, alone,
She takes her Ma'am's hand
Feels it warm in her own,
Then they talk and dream
Of Sissy's faraway home.
"She'll make her place with John Bee
And soon we'll be part of it too—
Then I'll make you a dress
On her porch in the sun,
One for all of the world to see!"

"An all−over dress?" Susannah asks,
"With a sash this wide and deep?
A rustle and bustle of all−over dress
And one that I can keep?"
Her Ma'am nods, "Yes, you can keep for all time,
And maybe another, real small and real fine."
Then she whispers something
And stares in the flame,
Susannah smiles her pleasure
As her Ma'am does the same.

"Blue sash, oh blue sash,
My sky blue, my true sash,
Wherever it is you may be,
My Ma'am hopes and prays
In that faraway home
There's a little one soon we shall see.

You binding us fast,
Our loving must last,
This good news my Ma'am just told to me—
That she's planning our Sissy a dress,
One for all of the world to see,
A waiting dress for a baby,
A baby who'll be born free!"

Nene Humphrey

A NOTE FROM THE ARTIST

My artwork comes from my mind; by that I mean I draw upon all my life experiences and filter them back out through my paintings and drawing. I try to hold on to everything I can remember happening in the past, and at the same time I'm always looking for new things to experience and add to my collection of remembrances. I often add collage materials to my paintings for emphasis. In doing the art for *Sky Sash So Blue*, I was challenged to show, while remaining true to the slave environment, how important Susannah's sash was to her, and the things she and her mother went through in order to get enough scraps to make Sissy's wedding dress.

For two remarkable sisters, Phyllis and Joyce
—L. H.

To Julian Denis Andrews
—B. A.

SIMON & SCHUSTER BOOKS FOR YOUNG READERS
An imprint of Simon & Schuster Children's Publishing Division
1230 Avenue of the Americas, New York, New York 10020
Text copyright © 1998 by Libby Hathorn
Illustrations copyright © 1998 by Benny Andrews
Book design by Lucille Chomowicz. The text for this book is set in Phaistos.
Printed and bound in the United States of America
First Edition 10 9 8 7 6 5 4 3 2 1
Library of Congress Cataloging-in-Publication Data
Hathorn, Elizabeth.
Sky sash so blue / by Libby Hathorn; illustrated by Benny Andrews
p. cm.
Summary: The special sky blue sash that a young slave girl offers to give her older sister
for her wedding dress becomes a tie that binds the family together when the sister moves away.
ISBN 0-689-81090-3 [1. Slavery–Fiction. 2. Afro-Americans–Fiction. 3. Stories in rhyme.]
I. Andrews, Benny, 1930– ill. II. Title PZ8.3.H287Sk 1998
[E]–dc21 96-53144 CIP AC